Ninnyhammer

"The master of animal adventures"
Independent on Sunday

"Sparkling humour and wonderful characters
are Dicking-Smith's trademarks"
Books for Your Children

"Dicking-Smith has brought magic into the
lives of millions of children"
Parents Magazine

"An author who has earned his stripes in the
world of animal writing so you know you'll be
in for a good read"
Belfast Telegraph

Also available by Dick King-Smith, award-winning
author and creator of *Babe*:

From Corgi Pups, for beginner readers
Happy Mouseday

From Young Corgi/Doubleday Books
The Adventurous Snail
All Because of Jackson
Billy the Bird
The Catlady
E.S.P.
Funny Frank
The Guard Dog
Hairy Hezekiah
Horse Pie
Titus Rules OK

From Corgi Yearling Books
Mr Ape
A Mouse Called Wolf
Harriet's Hare

From Corgi Books, for older readers
Godhanger
The Crowstarver

Dick King-Smith

Ninnyhammer

Illustrated by John Eastwood

Young Corgi

NINNYHAMMER

A YOUNG CORGI BOOK 978 0 552 55620 0

First published in Great Britain by Doubleday
an imprint of Random House Children's Books
A Random House Group Company

Doubleday edition published 2007
Young Corgi edition published 2008

3 5 7 9 10 8 6 4

The Random House Group Limited supports the Forest Stewardship
Council (FSC®), the leading international forest certification organisation.
Our books carrying the FSC label are printed on FSC® certified paper. FSC
is the only forest certification scheme endorsed by the leading environmental
organisations, including Greenpeace. Our paper procurement policy can be
found at www.randomhouse.co.uk/environment

MIX
Paper from
responsible sources
FSC® C013604

Set in PALATINO

Young Corgi Books are published by Random House Children's Books,
61–63 Uxbridge Road, London W5 5SA

www.kidsatrandomhouse.co.uk
www.randomhouse.co.uk

Addresses for companies within The Random House Group Limited can be found at:
www.randomhouse.co.uk/offices.htm

THE RANDOM HOUSE GROUP Limited Reg. No. 954009

A CIP catalogue record for this book is available from the British Library.

Printed and bound by CPI Group (UK) Ltd, Croydon, CR0 4YY

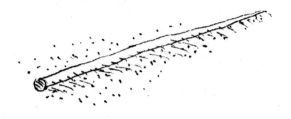

CHAPTER ONE

All his life Peter never forgot the date when he first spoke to Ninnyhammer. Mind you, it was a pretty easy date to remember – the first day of the first month of a new century.

Early on the morning of 1 January 1900 Peter had gone with his father to fetch the cows in for milking. Once they were all tied up in the cowshed, he walked down to the little stream that

ran through the farm. Here
and there it was crossed
by small wooden bridges;
Peter went to the nearest
one and stood on it,
leaning on the handrail.

He stared upstream,
hoping to see a kingfisher.
Instead, bobbing down towards
him on the surface of the clear water, he
saw something that at first looked like a small
straight stick. But when it floated closer, Peter
could see that it was white in colour and seemed
to be made of bone. As it passed under the
bridge, he noticed that it was tapered: one end
was as thick as a walking stick, the other as thin
as a pencil. But if it's not wood, Peter thought,
why doesn't it sink? Let's see if I can reach it.

He ran off the bridge and down to the edge
of the stream, a little way ahead of the floating
object. The stream was shallow and narrow, so he
waded into the water and managed to grab it.

At that moment he heard a loud shout and saw the figure of a big man hurrying down towards him. It's Ninnyhammer, he

thought. Peter sometimes saw the man around the village but had never spoken to him. He had often wondered who he was and where he lived. All he knew was what his father had told him: he was the village idiot.

"What's that mean, Father?" Peter had asked.

"He's simple," his father had said. "Soft in the head. 'Ninnyhammer' is an old word for someone like that."

"But where does he live?"

"I don't know. In the woods somewhere, I suppose. He keeps away from people; maybe the animals are his friends."

Now, when the big man reached Peter, he grunted something that sounded like "Hullo" and put out a hand, pointing at the stick that Peter was holding. There was a broad smile on his big bearded face, and Peter did not feel frightened or threatened.

"Is this yours?" he asked.

Ninnyhammer nodded a great many times. "Dropped it," he said in a deep voice. "In water. You give, boy?"

"Yes, of course," Peter replied, handing over the stick. "My name's Peter, by the way."

"Ninny-hammer," said the man. He reached out a large hand. "Ta, Pe-ter," he said, grinning happily.

"Please," Peter said, "what's it made of, that thing? It isn't wood, is it?"

Ninnyhammer shook his head a great many times.

"Well, what is it made of?"

"I-vor-y."

"Ivory? You mean, like an elephant's tusk?" asked Peter, and was answered by much nodding. "But then, that's bone. Why didn't it sink?"

Ninnyhammer laughed. He pointed the slender white stick at the boy. "Wand," he said.

Wand? thought Peter. What does he mean? Next he'll be telling me it's a magic wand.

"Keep secret, Pe-ter?" asked Ninnyhammer.

"Yes."

"Is ma-gic wand."

Told you so, said Peter to himself. He's soft in the head, he is.

"Show you," said Ninnyhammer.

Holding the wand by its thicker end, he pointed the thin end at the rippling, chuckling stream. "Stop!" he said loudly.

Immediately there was no more rippling, no more chuckling – no movement of water at all. Its surface was suddenly totally still. A twig that had been floating by was still. Further downstream, two ducks that had been swimming about were still. Nothing moved, in or on the water.

Peter looked at Ninnyhammer, who grinned at him.

"I don't understand," he said. "How could you possibly have stopped the stream like that?"

"Told you, Pe-ter. Is ma-gic."

Once again Ninnyhammer pointed his wand at the still water and said loudly, "Go!"

Instantly the stream rippled and chuckled once more; the twig floated away and the ducks swam off.

"Bye, Pe-ter," said Ninnyhammer, and he headed off upstream, swinging his magic wand. Then he stopped and turned and waved at Peter. "Keep secret," he called.

Peter walked back to the bridge and leaned on the handrail again, thinking, How could he possibly have stopped the water running? I must be dreaming. I'll pinch myself.

He pinched his arm, hard. It hurt.

Magic! he thought. But I can't see what else it could be. How exciting! Maybe Ninnyhammer can do anything with that wand. Maybe he could get me a pony, I've always wanted a pony but Father can't afford it.

Peter walked back up to the farm and went into the cowshed, where his father was sitting on his milking stool beside the final cow.

"Right, that's you done, Buttercup," said the farmer, and he got up, carried the bucket into the dairy and tipped the milk into the cooler.

"Guess what, Father," Peter said. "While you were milking the cows, I met Ninnyhammer."

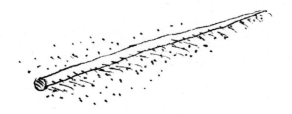

CHAPTER TWO

Farmer Frost felt the same as his neighbours. He didn't wish the simpleton any harm but he wasn't sure he wanted him appearing on his farm.

"Did he speak to you, Pete?" he asked.

"Yes."

"What did he say?"

"He said, 'Hullo.'"

"Brilliant," said Peter's father dryly. "He never says anything to me if I come across him."

"Does he smile at you, Father?"

"Smile? No, he's not like ordinary people. I told you, he's soft in the head."

That's what you think, Peter said to himself, remembering what Ninnyhammer had done with the magic wand. Nobody else in the world could do that. Father would never believe me if I told him how Ninnyhammer stopped the stream flowing and then started it again. But I'm not going to tell him. It's a secret between me and my . . . well, my friend, I suppose I could call him – my friend the wizard, because that's what he must be. I hope I meet him again soon.

*

But he didn't. Many weeks passed, during which Peter spent a lot of time – after school or at week-ends – searching all over the farm. He looked especially hard in the woods, where he thought his friend might have some sort of house – made of sticks perhaps. But he had no success.

"Father," he said at last, "d'you know where Ninnyhammer lives?"

"Lives?" said Farmer Frost. "I've no idea, Pete. I know he doesn't live in a house in the village or anywhere roundabout. He's not so keen on people and they're not as keen on him as you seem to be."

"Why's that?"

"Because he's strange, I suppose. He probably sleeps rough – under a hedge, like as not."

"But what if it's raining?"

"He gets wet."

I bet he doesn't, Peter thought. If that magic wand of his can stop a stream from running, then if it was raining, he'd just hold it up and say, "Stop, rain!" and it would. Or maybe he lives with the animals – the foxes keep dry in their earth, after all.

"Tell you one thing, Pete," said his father. "He's a tough old bird, Ninnyhammer is. He's been around for ages."

"Did you see him when you were a boy, Father?"

"Yes. But he never spoke to me."

That night Peter had a dream. He dreamed he was standing on the wooden bridge, leaning on the handrail, and suddenly, there was Ninnyhammer, standing on the bridge beside him. He was holding his wand in one hand and then he pointed it downstream.

The dream was so real that when Peter woke up, he lay wondering what it was that his friend had been pointing at.

The next day, a Saturday, Peter got up early and helped his father to bring in the cows for morning milking. Then – for there was time to kill before breakfast, which the Frosts ate after the milking was finished – Peter walked down to the stream and stood on the wooden bridge, leaning on the handrail. Then, suddenly, there was Ninnyhammer standing beside him, just as he'd done in the dream.

"Oh!" gasped Peter. "I didn't hear you coming!"

Ninnyhammer grinned. "Why you here, Peter?" he asked.

Because of a dream I had last night, Peter thought.

"I was hoping to see a kingfisher," he said.
"There's one that lives along this stretch of the
stream."

Then, just as he had done in the dream, the
wizard pointed his wand downstream, and at
the same time he cried in a high piping voice,
"Chee-chee-cheeky!"

Immediately the call was repeated from a bank further down the stream and, to Peter's amazement, the unmistakable shape of a kingfisher – large head, stumpy body, short wings and tail – came flying fast and low towards them.

"*Chee-ky!*" it cried as it skimmed above the water.

But when the bird reached the bridge, it did not fly under it and then off upstream, as Peter had thought it would, but instead landed right beside the wizard, clasping the handrail with its small bright-red feet.

"There!" said Ninny-hammer. With the tip of his ivory wand he stroked the little bird's brilliant blue-green back and then the chestnut underparts. "King-fisher for you, Pe-ter. You like?"

"Oh, Ninnyhammer!" Peter gasped. "Isn't it beautiful! Those colours! And a beak like a dagger. And to see it so close – that's magical!"

21

The wizard nodded many times, as usual. "Is mag-i-cal," he agreed, and he gently touched the sharp beak with the tip of his wand. "Go, friend," he said, and away the kingfisher flew.

Peter watched the bird till it was out of sight. "I do like birds," he said. "Well, I love all sorts of animals."

"You want to see fox?" Ninnyhammer asked.

"Oh yes! There's a fox's earth up there on the bank, near the path down from the farm. I sometimes hear it barking at night but I've never seen it."

Ninnyhammer pointed towards the bank with his wand. "Watch now, Pe-ter," he said, and at that very moment a red-coated, bushy-tailed creature came over the top. For a moment it stood quite still, looking down at the two figures on the bridge. Then it vanished into the mouth of the earth.

"Oh, Ninnyhammer!" Peter cried. "How lucky I am this morning. First the kingfisher and now the fox. Have you got lots of animal friends?"

"Yes. King-fisher my friend. Fox family is Ninny-hammer family. Fox-cubs my brothers," said the wizard. "But only one special friend, called Pe-ter." He looked down at the boy and smiled. "Ninny-hammer lose wand," he explained. "Pe-ter find in stream. Pe-ter ever need help, Ninny-hammer help him."

"Oh, thank you," said Peter. "But how shall I find you?"

"Pe-ter ever need me," said the wizard. "Come here to bridge."

"But how will you know I'm here?"

"Is ma-gic," said Ninnyhammer.

He reached out with his wand and touched

Peter on the shoulder. "Shut eyes. Pe-ter," he said. "Count to ten."

Peter did as he was told. He counted as quickly as he could, wondering what Ninnyhammer was going to do, but when he opened his eyes again, he was alone on the bridge.

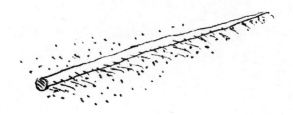

CHAPTER THREE

"I saw a fox just now," said Peter at breakfast. "It was on the bank above the stream, really near to me. It wasn't frightened."

"Guess who *I* saw," said his father.

"Who?"

"That old Ninnyhammer. I'd just turned the last cows out of the milking parlour and I looked up the yard and there he was, sitting on the fence."

"Did you say anything to him, Father?" Peter asked.

"Well, yes, I did. I was going to tell him to shove off, but he smiled at me – grinned all over his face in fact – and before I could say anything, he said, 'Morning, mister.'"

"And did you say good morning to him?" Peter's mother asked.

"Well, yes, I did, Sally."

"I'm glad you did, Jack."

"You'll never guess what the chap said then."

"What did he say?"

"He pointed at me with a kind of white stick he was carrying, and he said, 'Peter's daddy. Peter good boy,' and then he got off the fence and walked away. It's a funny thing, but when he pointed that stick at me, I suddenly felt happy. I don't mean I was unhappy before – I can't really

explain it . . . I just felt good about everything, and I was glad I hadn't told him to push off. What's more, I felt bad about how everyone treats the poor old fellow. I felt sort of guilty. After all, he can't help being the way he is."

"Perhaps it was a magic wand he pointed at you, Father," said Peter innocently.

"Magic wand!" said his father. "I only wish old Ninnyhammer was a magician. I could do with a bit of wizardry."

"Why, Father?"

"Well, it isn't as though this is a big farm, Pete. It's hard to make ends meet. If things don't get better, then before long we might have to—"

"Oh, don't bother Peter with business talk," his wife interrupted. "Here, tuck into this lot." And she handed her husband a plate of bacon and eggs.

Later, when his father had finished his breakfast and gone out into the yard, Peter said to his mother, "What did Father mean, about things not getting better?"

"Nothing for you to worry about, Peter," said his mother.

But I *am* worried, Peter said to himself. It sounds as if Father needs help. Then it suddenly  came to him: I know who could help! I was to come to the bridge if I needed him, Ninny-hammer said, and he'd know when I was there.

Perhaps Ninnyhammer could use his magic to help the farm, Peter thought. He'd be able to make the cows give more milk and the hens lay more eggs and the pigs have more piglets. Perhaps he could help with the weather too – make sure it didn't rain at haymaking or at harvest time. That must be easy for someone who could stop the stream from flowing with just one word.

Peter ran as fast as he could down to the bridge, past the bank where the fox's earth was, but there was no one there. He looked around but could see nobody. He walked out onto the bridge and waited. Be patient, he told himself. I'll try shutting my eyes and counting to ten, he thought, like I did when the wizard vanished.

This time he counted very slowly. He did not hear a sound, but when he opened his eyes, there was Ninnyhammer, wand in hand, standing beside him.

"What Peter want?" the wizard asked.

"You told me to say if I needed help," Peter said. "Well, I think it's my father who needs help."

"Mis-ter Jack Frost," said Ninnyhammer. "Money. Pe-ter's daddy needs more money."

How does he know that? Peter wondered. Well, he knows everything, I suppose. How strange that people think he's simple when he's really so wise.

"He was saying it was difficult to make ends meet," Peter said.

"Pe-ter not worry. Ninny-hammer help ends meet."

"How?"

"Ma-gic," said the wizard, and he set off for the nearby field, where Farmer Frost's herd of short-horn cows was grazing.

Watching from the bridge, Peter saw Ninny-hammer walk up to the nearest cow (who did not move away but stood quite still) and touch her with the magic wand. He was talking to her, Peter realized, though he could not hear the words.

Then the wizard moved on, stopping to touch and talk to each cow in turn. All stood quite still, listening carefully, it seemed, to what was being said.

Farmer Frost had twenty cows, and when Ninnyhammer had finished with the last of them, he turned and called to Peter, "More milk, more money!" Then he walked off over the hill and out of sight.

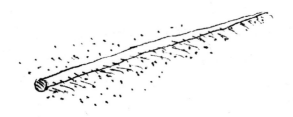

Chapter Four

Farmers are always grumbling about something or other. The weather's too hot or too cold, too wet or too dry; the cows aren't giving enough milk; the hens aren't laying enough eggs. Farmer Frost had always been a good grumbler, but suddenly he seemed more pleased with life.

"Something funny is going on, Sally," he said

to his wife at breakfast about a week later. "The cows are all giving quite a lot more milk. I recorded them yesterday and every cow's yield had gone up. I can't understand it."

"That's strange, Jack," said his wife. "My hens are laying like mad. I'm picking up almost twice as many eggs every day. I don't know why."

I do, thought Peter. It's my friend Ninnyhammer. More milk, more money; more eggs, more money. What next? I wonder.

"And the weather's been so good," said Farmer Frost. "Nice and warm and just enough rain. Everything's growing like mad. Come to think of it, things have been looking up ever since that old Ninnyhammer pointed his stick at me. Funny, that."

He smiled.

Sally Frost smiled too.

"Perhaps it *is* a magic wand," she said, "like Peter said."

Peter smiled. But he did not say anything.

39

That evening he went down to the footbridge and wasn't surprised to see that his friend the wizard was already there, leaning on the handrail, wand in hand.

Ninnyhammer greeted him with a broad smile. "Happy, Pe-ter?" he asked.

"Oh yes. Thank you, Ninnyhammer," Peter replied. He put out a hand. "Could I hold your wand just for a minute?" he asked.

"Yes," said Ninnyhammer, holding it out.

Peter took the wand. "It won't work for me, will it?" he said.

"Try it."

Holding the wand by its thicker end, Peter
pointed the thin end at the rippling, chuckling
stream. "Stop!" he said loudly.

Nothing happened, except that from a nearby
tree there came a loud laughing cry.

"What was that?" he asked.

The wizard smiled. "Woodpecker," he said.
"Thinks it funny."

"I'm silly," said Peter.
"Of course it only
works for you.
Father's cows are
giving more milk
– that's because you
touched them with
it, isn't it?"

Ninnyhammer nodded many times, as usual.
"Touched hens too," he
said.

"But how could
you do that?"

"Ma-gic," said the
wizard, grinning.
"Come on, Pe-ter.
We go see Father."
Farmer Frost was

sweeping out his yard when he saw them
coming. Peter, he could hear, was laughing
at something the simpleton had said. I'm
sure the old chap is a good man, he said to
himself. I'm certain of it. Wish I knew what
to call him – it doesn't feel right to call him what
everybody else does. Then suddenly he knew
how he should address him.

"Good morning, my friend," he said when they reached him, and he put down his yard broom and held out his hand.

Ninnyhammer shook it, holding his wand in his other hand and smiling a very broad smile. "Pe-ter friend to Ninny-hammer," he said. "Pe-ter's daddy too." And, as he had before, he pointed the wand at the farmer and again Jack Frost suddenly felt happy and carefree.

It's something to do with this funny old chap, the farmer thought. No wonder Peter likes him so much. I'd like to buy him a drink. And he put a hand in his pocket.

But even as he did so, Ninnyhammer said, "No thanks, Mis-ter Frost. Not need money." And he looked at Peter and gave him a big wink. "Ninny-hammer go now," he said. "Good-bye, Pe-ter. Goodbye, Mister Frost." Then he turned and walked off, swinging his wand.

The farmer picked up his broom. "He's nice, your friend, isn't he?" he said to his son.

"He's your friend too, Father. He said so," replied Peter.

Magic wand! thought Jack Frost as he began sweeping up the muck again. What a lot of nonsense! Cows giving more milk, hens laying more eggs – how could that have anything to do with old Ninnyhammer? Still, I'd quite like to do something for the old fellow. I've certainly felt better about everything since he's been around the place – I'm sure I don't know why.

"Have a think, Sally," he said to his wife when he went in for his tea. "What could I do for Peter's friend?"

"Ninnyhammer, you mean? Why don't you give him some money, Jack. I shouldn't think he's got much."

"I was going to give him the price of a drink but he said he didn't want it."

Sally Frost looked out of the window. It was

beginning to rain hard. "I dare say he'd be glad of a roof over his head, especially in weather like this."

"Have him live with us, here in the farmhouse? You can't mean that," said Jack Frost, thinking of Ninnyhammer's filthy old clothes and dirty boots.

"No. But there are plenty of roofs around the farmyard. He could use the barn perhaps. He'd be in the dry and he could sleep on the straw. He'd be as snug as a bug in a rug."

"He might not like the idea."

"Ask him."

"Tell you what," said Farmer Frost. "I'll get Pete to ask him."

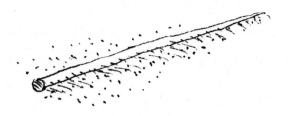

CHAPTER FIVE

Peter could not bring himself to tell Ninny-hammer that he could shelter in the barn or one of the other farm buildings. Somehow he felt embarrassed offering him a barn to sleep in. He felt sure that Ninnyhammer had a magical home down in the ground with his fox family. Although he wouldn't have much room there.

For some weeks he did not go down to the

bridge, but then a spell of heavy rain set in, and he kept saying, to himself, Surely even wizards must get soaked if they've no roof over their heads?

"Seen old Ninnyhammer lately?" Peter's father asked one morning.

"No, Father."

"Poor old fellow. He must be wringing wet all day and night."

I've *got* to tell him, Peter thought. I've just *got* to.

So next morning he set off down towards the bridge.

It was a beautiful sunny morning, the sort that makes everyone feel pleased with life, especially after a wet spell.

As he walked along, something happened that made Peter feel even happier. He looked up at the bank where the fox's earth was, hoping for a glimpse of that bushy-tailed, prick-eared creature, and there, tumbling about in play just outside the mouth of the earth, were four fox cubs.

Peter could hear the fierce little growls of their mock-fighting, and as he listened, he heard too the loud laughing cry of the woodpecker, the cawing of rooks, the cooing of wood-pigeons, the chattering of magpies and the *"Chee-chee-cheeky!"* call of the kingfisher, as though all the birds on the farm were celebrating the appearance of the cubs. He was so excited to see Ninnyhammer's "family"!

Finally, as Peter neared the bridge, he heard the cows mooing loudly. Looking up the opposite slope, he saw Ninnyhammer coming down, wand in one hand while with the other he patted the muzzle of one of the cows, which was walking beside him like a dog.

It was Buttercup, the leader of the herd. She fell back as the wizard reached the little bridge, and all the other cows joined her, still mooing loudly.

Ninnyhammer turned and pointed his wand at the herd. "Quiet, please," he said, and instantly they all fell silent, walked down to the stream and began to drink.

"Good mor-ning, Pe-ter," the wizard said.

"Oh, it *is* a good morning, Ninnyhammer," cried Peter. "The sun's out, all the birds sound happy, and the cows do too. They like you – anyone can see that. And what d'you think I saw on the way down?"

"Four fox cubs," replied Ninnyhammer. "Playing in the sun. I knew they would come out today."

"The weather's been awful lately, hasn't it?" Peter said. But your clothes don't look very wet, he thought. Perhaps you *have* got shelter somewhere. I must offer you shelter, though – Father told me to.

"Would you like to walk back up to the farm with me?" he asked. "There's something I need to talk to you about."

A big grin spread over Ninnyhammer's bearded face, and he nodded, many times.

It's almost as if he knows what I'm going to say, Peter thought. As they set off up the path, he wondered whether the fox cubs would still be out.

"They will be," said Ninnyhammer, as though Peter had spoken his thoughts out loud, and they were.

At the sight of the wizard they stopped their rough-and-tumble and sat in a line, staring down at him. Peter thought he could see

their little brushes waving, like puppies' tails. It almost seemed as if they were smiling at Ninnyhammer.

I hope Father's in the yard, Peter said to himself. Then he can ask my friend if he'd like some shelter. But as they approached, he saw that the two big plough horses were not in the stable, and knew that he must go through with it alone.

In the barn he turned to face the wizard. "Ninnyhammer,"

he said, "I don't want to seem rude, but if you've nowhere to shelter when it's raining, you'd be very welcome to come in here."

"Mis-ter Frost say so?" asked Ninnyhammer.

"Yes."

Ninnyhammer grinned even more widely. He pointed with his wand at the stack of straw that almost filled one half of the barn. "Sleep up there?" he said.

"Yes," answered Peter. "It's not like having a proper bed, I know, but it's better than being out in the rain."

Tucking his wand under one arm, Ninny-hammer began to climb the long ladder that stood against the straw-stack. When he reached the top, he looked down and said, "Pe-ter come up too?"

Oh, crumbs, thought Peter! It's an awfully long ladder and I don't much like heights.

"Come on, brave boy," said the wizard and pointed his wand at Peter.

Immediately Peter felt that of course he could go up the ladder, and he began to climb.

As he reached the top, the wizard began to laugh loudly.

"What's funny?" Peter asked.

For answer Ninnyhammer pointed to the straw at the top of the stack. Peter could see a hollow in it; a hollow the size of a big man; a hollow that someone had made to sleep in, out of the rain, in the warm.

"Ninny-hammer's bed," said the wizard.

"You've already been sleeping here!" Peter gasped. "All through this wet weather?"

Ninnyhammer nodded and nodded. "Kind Mis-ter Frost," he said. "Told Pe-ter, Ask your friend. Foxes kind to Ninny-hammer, but real home better. Thank you."

"But how did you know what Father said?" Peter asked.

Ninnyhammer grinned. He pulled at his beard and raised his bushy eyebrows and waved his ivory wand.

Peter smiled happily. "I know what you're going to say," he said.

"What?"

"Magic."

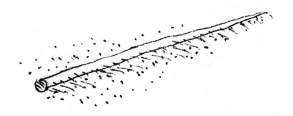

Chapter Six

"Guess what," Peter said to his father that evening. "While you were out ploughing, I met Ninnyhammer."

"Oh, good," said Farmer Frost. "Did you ask him if he fancied sleeping in the barn sometimes?"

"Yes," Peter replied.

"And did he like the idea?"

"Oh yes. He said it was very kind of you."

"I told you he'd be glad of a roof over his head," Sally Frost said to her husband. "Poor old chap, he must have been soaking wet these last few nights. Now he'll be as snug as a bug in a rug, like I said. Anyway, I'm half beginning to believe that he *does* bring us luck somehow. More eggs, more milk. What next?"

"More piglets perhaps," said Jack Frost. "Old Molly is due to farrow any time now. She's never had more than eight in a litter but it wouldn't surprise me if she had more – even twelve – if old Ninnyhammer tapped her with his stick."

"His magic wand, d'you mean, Father?" said Peter, and his parents smiled at one another.

"Bedtime for you, Peter," said his mother.

"Can I just go up to the barn first?" he asked.

"Why?"

"To say goodnight to Ninnyhammer."

"No, Pete," said Farmer Frost. "The old chap might have gone to bed early now he's got somewhere warm and dry to sleep."

I'll go up there first thing in the morning, Peter thought as he lay in bed. I hope Molly doesn't farrow tonight though. Then he went to sleep and dreamed that he was out walking on the farm with Ninnyhammer when the wizard pointed his wand at something and said, "Pot of gold."

Peter woke up very early the next morning, even before his father had gone out to bring the cows in for milking. He got dressed and went straight over to Molly's sty and peeped in. The old sow was lying on her side. She gave a sleepy grunt but did not get up.

She looks enormous, Peter thought. I wouldn't be surprised if she *does* have twelve babies. Which she will if I get Ninnyhammer to help.

He went into the barn and stood at the foot of the long ladder and called very softly, "Ninny-hammer? Are you asleep?"

The only answer from above was a loud snore.

Peter waited a bit and then repeated his question, rather more loudly. The snoring stopped, and a few moments later a big bearded face peered over the top of the stack and grinned down at him.

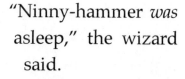

"Ninny-hammer *was* asleep," the wizard said.

"Oh, sorry," said Peter. "You know, I had a funny dream about you last night. You pointed your wand at something and said . . . well, it sounded like 'Pot of gold.' What could that have meant?"

"Rain-bow," said the wizard.

"Rainbow?"

"Ask Father."

"Oh. Look, I wanted to ask you something."

"What Pe-ter want?"

"Well, you know our sow Molly – in the sty down at the bottom of the yard?"

Ninnyhammer nodded many times, as usual.

"Well, she's due any time now, and I wondered – d'you think you could tap her tummy with your wand?"

Down the ladder came the wizard, nodding and grinning, and they walked down to the pigsty together.

Molly got up as they entered, and Ninny-hammer began to scratch her back with the thicker end of his wand. The sow stood snuffling and grunting softly with what sounded like great pleasure.

"All animals like you, don't they?" Peter said.

"Ninny-hammer like all ani-mals," replied the wizard.

"Please," Peter said, "can you tap her tummy with your wand? Maybe then she'll have as many piglets as you give her taps. She's never had more than eight, but Father thinks you could make her have twelve."

"Mis-ter Frost believe in ma-gic?"

"Not yet. But perhaps he will do one day."

Ninnyhammer stopped scratching the sow's back and very gently began to tap the side of her big belly. Each time, the sow grunted softly, and after twelve grunts she turned away and went back to lie on her bed of straw.

At that moment Farmer Frost came into the yard, on his way to bring his cows in for milking.

"Good morning, my friend," he said to Ninnyhammer. "I trust you slept well?"

After much nodding the wizard said, "Ninny-hammer thank Mis-ter Frost."

"Don't mention it," said the farmer.

He looked over the wall of the pigsty. "She shouldn't be long now," he said.

"To-night," said Ninnyhammer.

"Oh, really? Next thing, you'll be telling me how many piglets she's going to have."

"Twelve," said the wizard.

The farmer smiled. "I hope you're right, my friend," he said, "but it'll be a miracle if you are. The old girl's never had more than eight."

And he walked off into the field beyond, calling, "Cow! Cow! Cow!"

"Of course you'll be right, Ninnyhammer," Peter said. "And then I won't be the only person in our family who believes in magic."

As soon as Peter woke next morning, very early again, he pulled on his clothes and his boots and ran down to the pigsty.

Inside lay Molly, suckling twelve piglets.

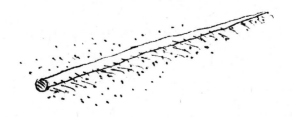

CHAPTER SEVEN

"That Ninnyhammer . . ." said Jack Frost to his wife later that day, "He *is* a magician – a wizard – call it what you will. I'm sure of that now, Sally."

"Me too," replied his wife. "He tells you that old Molly will have twelve piglets and she does. We're very lucky to have him around, I think."

"Maybe Pete's right about that stick the old

chap carries; maybe it *is* a magic wand."

"So now you believe in magic, do you, Jack?"

Peter came into the room in time to hear his mother's question. "Do you, Father?" he said.

"Sort of. I believe our friend Ninnyhammer has some very special gifts."

"Oh, that reminds me," Peter said. "He told me to ask you about rainbows. Something about a pot of gold . . ."

"Oh, that!" laughed his father. "That's just an old saying: there's supposed to be a pot of gold at the end of a rainbow. If you can see the end. Which you never can."

Spring turned into summer, and haymaking began. The weather was perfect throughout, and with the help of a couple of men from the village, Farmer Frost made a lot of good hay. The two big horses pulled in cartload after cartload, and by the end of June there was a huge haystack at the top of the yard.

"First of July tomorrow," Sally Frost said to her husband that night.

"I know that. So what?"

"Only that Peter's birthday is getting near."

"I know. July the tenth."

"When he will be ten."

"I know that too, Sally."

"But do you know what he wants?"

"Why, has he told you?"

"Yes. He wants a pony."

"A pony!" cried Jack Frost. "That'd cost a fortune. I'm not made of money, you know."

"Oh, all right! Buy him a packet of licorice."

While he was milking his cows next morning,

Farmer Frost tried to figure out how he could afford what Peter wanted. Even with the extra money he was getting now that Ninnyhammer was making his cows produce more milk, his hens lay more eggs and his sow have twelve piglets, it was still a stretch. It wasn't just the price of the animal. There was the tack it would need – a saddle alone cost pounds and pounds – and then there was its keep. I could borrow some money, I suppose, he thought, but who from? Who could help me?

At that very moment the large figure of Ninnyhammer came quietly into the cowshed Buttercup gave a low moo of pleasure, and all the other cows followed suit.

"Good mor-ning, Mis-ter Frost," said the wizard, pointing his wand at the farmer, and instantly Jack Frost felt that somehow he need worry no more; somehow he would be able to get Peter his pony.

"Good morning, my friend," he replied. "What can I do for you?"

"Not worry," Ninnyhammer said. "Mis-ter Frost not worry about present for Pe-ter." Then he turned and went out of the cowshed.

He *is* a wizard, Jack Frost thought.

He finished milking the last cow, Buttercup, carried the pail up to the dairy and poured the milk into the cooler. He looked out of the dairy door and then up at the sky, and there was a rainbow! It was a big rainbow that arched out of the sky and curved down to end close by, in the orchard next to the yard.

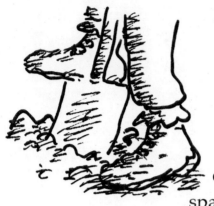

A voice in the farmer's head said, *Quick, get a spade!* So he did. Then *Dig where you saw the rainbow end.* So he did, and there was a clanking noise as the spade struck something in the ground. *Dig it out!* said the voice, so he did.

Under the turf was a rusty old tin box, and when Jack Frost knelt in the grass, lifted it out and opened it up, he was somehow not in the least surprised to find that it was full of golden guineas.

"Enough for pony?"
said a deep voice, and
he looked up to see
Ninnyhammer
grinning down
at him.

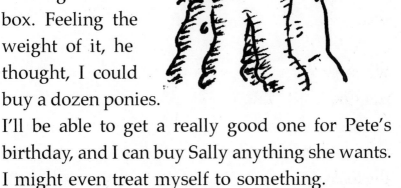

Jack Frost
got to his feet,
holding the
box. Feeling the
weight of it, he
thought, I could
buy a dozen ponies.
I'll be able to get a really good one for Pete's
birthday, and I can buy Sally anything she wants.
I might even treat myself to something.

"Thank you, my friend," he said to the
wizard.

Ninnyhammer grinned even more widely and pulled at his beard and raised his bushy eyebrows and waved his magic wand.

You know everything, don't you? thought the farmer. You probably know who buried this box many years ago, and you somehow made the rainbow end here. But you mustn't tell Peter – I want the pony to be a surprise.

"Ninny-hammer not tell Pe-ter," said the wizard, and he turned and walked away.

On 8 July 1901 Farmer Jack Frost, his pockets bulging with golden guineas, got out his old bicycle (I must get myself a new one, he thought) and cycled off to market. There he bought an Exmoor pony, a lovely, sturdy, brown filly, and arranged for her to be delivered to his farm on the following Sunday, 10 July.

On the Saturday Peter walked down to the old wooden bridge, hoping to meet Ninnyhammer. He looked up at the fox's earth even though he knew Ninnyhammer wouldn't be there any longer. There was nothing to see, for the cubs had grown up and left. As he neared the bridge, he heard the familiar *"Cheee-chee-cheeky!"* call and saw the kingfisher flashing upstream.

Standing on the bridge, wand in hand, was the wizard.

"Hullo, Pe-ter," said Ninnyhammer. "To-morrow is birth-day, eh?"

"Yes."

"Mis-ter Frost give Pe-ter nice present?"

"I don't know," Peter said. "What I really want is a pony of my own, but I don't think Father could afford it. They're very expensive."

Ninnyhammer nodded a great many times, but he had a special big smile on his face. I wonder why, thought Peter.

All his long life Peter Frost never forgot the morning of his tenth birthday. At first all his mother and father said to him was, "Happy birthday!" But then they said, "After breakfast you can have your present."

"Can't I have it now?"

"No, it's too big."

Too big, thought Peter. Could it be . . . ? Yes, it could, he told himself, if Ninnyhammer had anything to do with it!

He bolted his breakfast and then they all went up to the stables, and there, in a little stall next to the two big carthorses, was a beautiful brown Exmoor pony.

"Many happy returns!" said Peter's parents.

"Oh, isn't she lovely!" Peter cried. "Oh, thank you so much!"

At that moment a deep voice behind them said, "Hap-py birth-day, Pe-ter."

"Thank you, Ninnyhammer."

"Yes," said Jack Frost. "You certainly should thank our friend."

"Yes," said Peter, stroking the pony's neck in a daze of happiness. "But what shall I call her?"

"I'm sure Ninnyhammer will suggest a good name," said Sally Frost.

"Go on then, Ninnyhammer," said Peter. "Please."

The wizard grinned and nodded, and then he said, "Pe-ter call her Ma-gic."

THE END